The baker and his wife decided to bake up a new treat,
Maybe try a special recipe that Santa would like to eat!

When the cookies were baked, and the frosting was done,
They ate the whole tray of samples, all but one.

Well, Gary was the last gingerbread man left on the plate,
And if he didn't think of an escape, it would be too late.

That night, the Baker and his wife went up to their warm bed,
Dreams about eating the last cookie danced around in their head.

Gary got up and called the Muffin Man,
He said, "Hurry! Come help me as fast as you can!
How do I keep from smelling so delicious?
I want to stay alive, without looking suspicious."

The Muffin Man tells him, "Gary, you just smell so yummy.
You need to stink so bad, they feel sick to their tummy.
Eat out of the garbage, it is a fine place to start,
Surely, by morning, you will have the worst farts."

So, Gary did just as he was told,
He ate some garbage, some new and some old.

Within an hour, his belly filled with bubbly gas,
He lifted his leg and let the stinker pass.

For breakfast, the Baker and his wife wanted something to eat,
Maybe some coffee and to share something sweet.

They came out of their room and covered their noses,
The Baker said, "Ugh! It smells like the sewer exploded!"

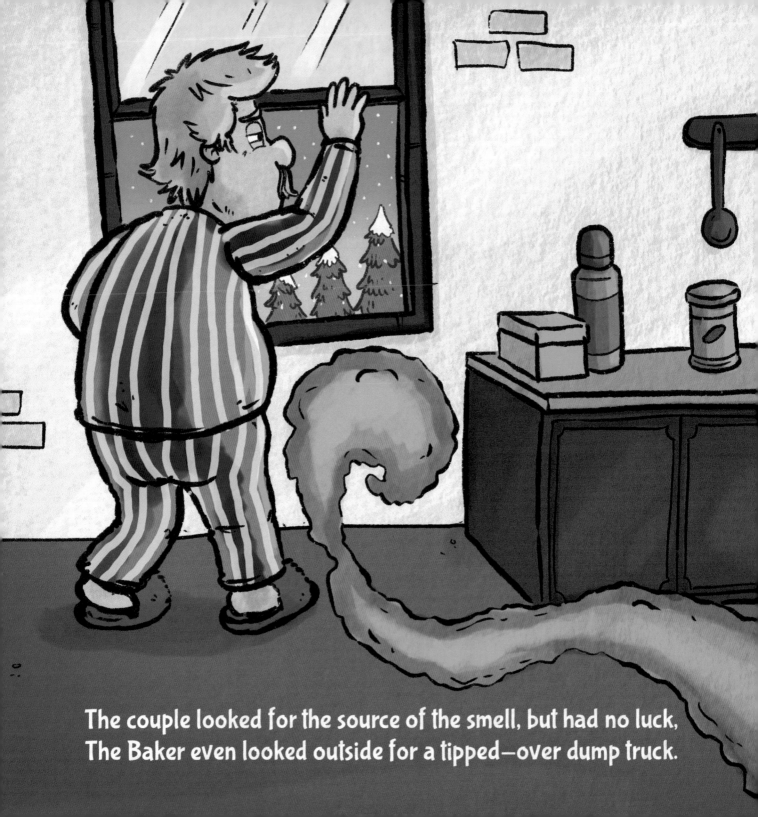

The couple looked for the source of the smell, but had no luck,
The Baker even looked outside for a tipped—over dump truck.

Gary's plan was working, of this he had no doubt,
They would see he was the smell and simply throw him out.

He would run away to the woods, and live in the trees,
Become friends with the butterflies, beetles, and bees.

He could lay in the sun and play in the sand,
And hang out with his friend, the Muffin Man.

The Baker's wife sniffed Gary and quickly became upset,
The cookie was the smelly culprit, and it made her depressed!

She could have eaten him in two big bites,
Instead, he became spoiled sitting overnight.

She looked at him closer, and Gary was in trouble,
That gas in his belly was starting to bubble.

Gary filled with more air, and the Baker gave him a poke,
The smell that came out, almost made them both choke.

This was it, Gary's time to escape!
He stood up and jumped off of the plate.

The gas clouds were thick, time to explore!
Gary had to find his way to the front door.

The Baker's dog ran in to see what was the matter,
Gary grabbed her collar and used it as a ladder.

The dog ran right towards the woods, much to his surprise.
He knew that he was free, once they got outside.

Gary made it to a tree and climbed up its bark,
He sat on a branch until the sky got dark.

The cookie smiled as he completed his plan,
He would soon be rescued by his friend, the Muffin Man.

Dear reader,

Thank you so much for purchasing and reading this book. It would mean the world to me as an author if you shared your impressions. Please take two minutes to share your review on Amazon with the millions of parents and children (and me!) who are waiting for your valued feedback.

Yours truly,
Tom

Printed in Great Britain
by Amazon